The Impact Chronicles

Seeds of Renewal: Love's Everlasting Bloom

The Impact Chronicles, Volume 4

Paul Smith

Published by Paul Smith, 2024.

SEEDS OF RENEWAL: LOVE'S EVERLASTING BLOOM

First edition. February 23, 2024.

ISBN: 979-8224100170

Written by Paul Smith.

Table of Contents

In dedication to my late father Malcolm Smith - 49-2020 from Parkinson's disease, so every little helps goes a long way eventually.

Book 4, "Seeds of Renewal: Love's Everlasting Bloom,"

Book 4, "Seeds of Renewal: Love's Everlasting Bloom," shifts focus to Emily and

Adam as they navigate the complexities of love, loss, and renewal. Through their

journey, they discover that love has the power to heal wounds, ignite passions, and

inspire transformation, reminding them of the enduring hope that lies within each

new beginning.

The Impact Chronicles

Title: "Seeds of Renewal: Love's Everlasting Bloom"

Summary: In the fourth installment of the "Impact Chronicles" series, "Seeds of Renewal," we follow Emily and Adam as they navigate the next chapter of their lives, filled with love, purpose, and new challenges.

As the founders of the thriving shop and gallery, "Renewal," Emily and Adam have established themselves as pillars of their community, inspiring others with their commitment to environmental sustainability and social justice. Together, they continue to cultivate a space where creativity flourishes and ideas blossom, fostering connections and driving positive change.

Amidst the hustle and bustle of their business, Emily and Adam find themselves facing unexpected hurdles, from financial setbacks to personal conflicts. However, their love and resilience only grow stronger as they confront these challenges head-on, united in their determination to overcome any obstacle.

Meanwhile, a new opportunity arises that could take their impact to new heights: a chance to collaborate on a large-scale environmental restoration project in their coastal town. As they immerse themselves in this ambitious endeavor, Emily and Adam discover the true depth of their connection and the power of love to fuel their shared mission.

Through their journey of renewal, Emily and Adam inspire those around them to embrace change, adapt to adversity, and never lose sight of the seeds of hope that lie within each challenge. Their story reminds us that love, when nurtured with compassion and purpose, has the power to transform not only our lives but also the world around us.

"Seeds of Renewal: Love's Everlasting Bloom" is a heartwarming tale of love, resilience, and the enduring power of hope, reminding us that even in the face of uncertainty, the seeds of renewal are always within reach.

so after Adam lost his father to an awful disease and because his dad did not get to see his love of fish is built what he thought was his dreams so show his children anything is possible so it was the fish that saved them in the end.

The Impact Chronicles

Contents

The Impact Chronicles

Book 4

Chapter 1: A New Horizon

As the sun rose over the horizon, casting a warm glow over the sleepy town of Ramsey, Adam
and Emily stood at the edge of the coastline, gazing out at the tranquil sea. It had been a long
journey to get here, but as they took in the salty breeze and the sound of seagulls overhead, they
knew that they had finally found a place to call home.

For Adam, Ramsey represented a fresh start—a chance to leave behind the hustle and bustle of
city life and reconnect with his passion for marine life. Ever since he was a child, he had been
fascinated by the mysteries of the ocean, spending hours exploring tide pools and studying fish
in aquariums. Now, with Ramsey's picturesque shores stretching out before him, he felt a sense
of peace and belonging that he had been longing for.

Beside him, Emily's eyes sparkled with excitement as she took in the beauty of their new
surroundings. While she wasn't as well-versed in the world of fish as Adam, she shared his
enthusiasm for their new adventure. Together, they had dreamed of starting a new life—a life

filled with purpose, creativity, and the joy of making a difference in their community.

As they walked hand in hand along the sandy shore, Adam and Emily knew that the road ahead

wouldn't be easy. They would face challenges and obstacles along the way, but they were ready

to confront them head-on, fueled by their love for each other and their shared vision for the

future.

With the sun shining brightly overhead and the promise of a new day dawning, Adam and Emily

took their first steps into the unknown, eager to see where this new chapter would take them.

Little did they know, their journey was only just beginning, and the adventures that lay ahead

would shape their lives in ways they could never have imagined.

Chapter 2: Finding Their Footing

As the days turned into weeks, Adam and Emily worked tirelessly to settle into their new home in

Ramsey. Their cozy cottage, nestled among the rolling hills overlooking the sea, quickly became

a sanctuary—a place where they could unwind after long days of exploration and adventure.

Together, they ventured out to explore their new surroundings, immersing themselves in the

vibrant community of Ramsey. They frequented local cafes and shops, eager to connect with

their neighbors and learn more about life on the island.

Despite their initial excitement, however, they soon realized that building a new life wouldn't be

without its challenges. The cost of living was higher than they had anticipated, and finding stable

employment proved to be more difficult than they had hoped.

But Adam and Emily refused to be discouraged. They knew that their dreams were worth fighting

for, and they were determined to make them a reality. With Adam's background in marine biology

and Emily's expertise in online marketing, they began to brainstorm ideas for a business that

would not only support them financially but also allow them to pursue their passions.

As they sat together in their cozy cottage, surrounded by the comforting scent of sea air and the

sound of waves crashing against the shore, Adam and Emily felt a renewed sense of purpose.

They knew that they were exactly where they were meant to be, and that no matter what

challenges lay ahead, they would face them together, hand in hand, as they embarked on this new chapter of their lives.

Chapter 3: Weathering the Storm

As autumn descended upon Ramsey, a sense of anticipation hung in the air. The island's
residents braced themselves for the unpredictable weather that often accompanied the changing
seasons, but nothing could have prepared them for the ferocity of the storm that was about to
strike.

Dark clouds gathered on the horizon, obscuring the sun and casting a shadow over the town. The
wind howled through the streets, bending trees and sending debris flying in its wake. Waves
crashed against the shore with a deafening roar, threatening to breach the seawall and inundate
the lower town.

Adam and Emily watched anxiously from their cottage window as the storm raged outside. They
had heard warnings of high tides and strong winds, but nothing could have prepared them for the
sheer force of nature unleashed upon their tranquil island home.

As the storm intensified, the power flickered and died, plunging the town into darkness. Adam
and Emily huddled together, listening to the sound of the wind and rain battering against the
walls of their cottage. In that moment, they felt a sense of vulnerability unlike anything they had

ever experienced before.

Hours passed, each one feeling like an eternity, until finally, the storm began to subside. Adam

and Emily emerged from their shelter, cautiously stepping outside to survey the damage. The

streets were littered with debris, and the lower town had been hit particularly hard by the rising

tide.

But amidst the destruction, there was also a glimmer of hope. Neighbors emerged from their

homes, ready to lend a helping hand to those in need. Together, they began the arduous task of

clearing away fallen trees and debris, determined to rebuild their community stronger than ever

before.

As Adam and Emily joined their fellow residents in the cleanup efforts, they felt a renewed sense

of purpose. The storm may have tested their resolve, but it had also brought them closer

together, forging bonds of friendship and resilience that would endure long after the clouds had

cleared.

Chapter 4: A Beacon of Light

In the aftermath of the storm, Ramsey's residents came together to assess the damage and

begin the process of rebuilding. Adam and Emily, determined to contribute to the community's

recovery, offered their assistance wherever it was needed.

One morning, as they walked through the town surveying the damage, they stumbled upon a

dilapidated building nestled among the rubble. Despite its worn exterior, Adam saw potential in

the building's spacious layout and prime location in the heart of town.

With Emily's encouragement, Adam shared his vision for the building—a place where locals and

tourists alike could gather to learn about marine life and the importance of environmental

conservation. Inspired by their shared passion, they decided to embark on a new venture:

transforming the building into a gallery and sea life sanctuary.

Word of their ambitious project quickly spread throughout the town, sparking excitement and

enthusiasm among Ramsey's residents. Neighbors offered their support and expertise, eager to

help bring Adam and Emily's vision to life.

Together, they worked tirelessly to renovate the building, painting walls, installing tanks, and creating immersive exhibits that showcased the beauty and diversity of marine life. With each

passing day, the gallery began to take shape, becoming a beacon of hope and renewal in the

wake of the storm.

As the grand opening approached, Adam and Emily felt a sense of pride and accomplishment

unlike anything they had ever experienced before. Their journey had been filled with challenges

and setbacks, but they had never lost sight of their dream. And now, as they stood on the

threshold of a new beginning, they knew that their efforts had been worth it.

As the doors of the gallery swung open for the first time, Ramsey's residents gathered to

celebrate the culmination of months of hard work and dedication. For Adam and Emily, it was a

moment of triumph—a testament to the power of resilience, community, and the enduring hope

that lies within each of us.

Chapter 5: Seeds of Inspiration

With the gallery and sea life sanctuary now open to the public, Adam and Emily found themselves

immersed in a whirlwind of activity. Visitors from near and far flocked to Ramsey to marvel at the

stunning exhibits and learn about the wonders of the ocean.

As they walked through the gallery, Adam and Emily couldn't help but feel a sense of pride at

what they had accomplished. Each tank teemed with life, showcasing a diverse array of marine

creatures, from colorful coral reefs to majestic sea turtles.

But beyond the beauty of the exhibits, Adam and Emily saw something even more powerful at

work—the spark of inspiration ignited in the eyes of their visitors. Children gasped in awe as they

watched fish darting through the water, while adults lingered over informational displays, eager to

learn more about conservation efforts and environmental sustainability.

For Adam and Emily, the gallery wasn't just a place to display marine life—it was a platform for

education and advocacy, a space where they could share their passion for the ocean and inspire

others to take action to protect it.

As they watched the gallery come to life with each passing day, Adam and Emily felt a sense of fulfillment unlike anything they had ever experienced before. Their dream had evolved from a

simple desire to share their love of fish into something much larger—a movement to create

positive change in their community and beyond.

And as they looked to the future, Adam and Emily knew that the seeds of inspiration they had

planted in Ramsey would continue to grow and flourish, shaping the hearts and minds of

generations to come.

Chapter 6: Community Connections

As the gallery and sea life sanctuary flourished, Adam and Emily found themselves woven even

deeper into the fabric of Ramsey's tight-knit community. Their venture had become more than

just a business—it was a gathering place, a hub of activity where neighbors came together to

connect and share in their love of the ocean.

Local artists showcased their work in the gallery's exhibition space, drawing visitors from far and

wide to admire their talent and creativity. Fish enthusiasts exchanged tips and stories in the

gallery's cozy café, bonding over their shared passion for marine life.

But perhaps most importantly, the gallery provided a space for education and outreach, hosting

workshops, lectures, and community events aimed at raising awareness about marine

conservation and environmental stewardship. Children gathered for hands-on activities and

guided tours, learning about the importance of protecting our oceans for future generations.

Adam and Emily were heartened by the positive response their efforts received from the

community. They had set out to create a space where people could come together to learn, explore, and be inspired, and seeing their vision come to life filled them with a profound sense of

gratitude and purpose.

As they watched the gallery buzz with activity each day, Adam and Emily knew that they were

part of something special—a movement to foster connection, curiosity, and compassion in their

corner of the world. And as they looked ahead to the future, they felt hopeful that their gallery

would continue to serve as a beacon of light and inspiration for years to come.

Chapter 7: Building Dreams

With the gallery and sea life sanctuary thriving, Adam and Emily began to dream even bigger.

Inspired by the success of their initial venture, they started to envision new ways they could make

a positive impact on their community and beyond.

One evening, as they sat together in their cozy cottage overlooking the sea, Adam shared an idea

that had been brewing in his mind for some time. He spoke passionately about his vision for a

larger-scale sea life center—a place where visitors could immerse themselves in the wonders of

the ocean through interactive exhibits, educational programs, and conservation initiatives.

Emily listened intently, her eyes shining with excitement. She had always admired Adam's

passion for marine biology and conservation, and she could see how much this project meant to

him. Together, they began to brainstorm ideas for how they could turn Adam's vision into a reality.

They reached out to experts in the field, seeking advice and guidance on how to design and fund

such an ambitious project. They also engaged with the local community, hosting town hall

meetings and gathering feedback from residents about what they would like to see in a sea life center.

As they worked tirelessly to bring their dream to fruition, Adam and Emily encountered their fair

share of challenges and setbacks. They faced logistical hurdles, financial constraints, and even

moments of doubt. But through it all, they remained steadfast in their belief that they could make

a difference.

With each passing day, their vision began to take shape, fueled by their passion and

determination. And as they looked ahead to the future, Adam and Emily knew that they were on

the cusp of something truly extraordinary—a legacy that would endure for generations to come.

Chapter 8: Community Support

As Adam and Emily's vision for the sea life center gained momentum, they were overwhelmed by

the outpouring of support from the community. Neighbors, local businesses, and organizations

rallied behind their cause, offering their expertise, resources, and financial backing to help bring

the project to life.

The gallery and sea life sanctuary had become a beloved fixture in Ramsey, drawing visitors from

near and far and serving as a testament to Adam and Emily's commitment to marine

conservation. Now, the community was eager to see their dream of a larger-scale sea life center

become a reality.

Volunteers rolled up their sleeves to assist with fundraising efforts, organizing bake sales, charity

events, and community auctions to generate funds for the project. Local businesses offered

sponsorships and donations, recognizing the positive impact the sea life center would have on

tourism and the local economy.

Even Ramsey's youngest residents got involved, organizing school fundraisers and awareness

campaigns to support the cause. Their enthusiasm and passion inspired others to join the effort, spreading the message of marine conservation far and wide.

Adam and Emily were humbled by the outpouring of generosity and support from their

community. It was a testament to the power of collaboration and collective action, demonstrating

what could be achieved when people came together with a shared purpose.

As they continued to work towards their goal, Adam and Emily knew that they were not alone in

their quest. They were surrounded by a community of caring and compassionate individuals who

believed in their vision and were committed to making it a reality. And with their support, they

knew that anything was possible.

Chapter 9: Facing Challenges

As the plans for the sea life center progressed, Adam and Emily encountered a series of

unexpected challenges that tested their resolve and determination.

One of the biggest obstacles they faced was securing the necessary funding to finance the

construction and operation of the center. Despite their best efforts to raise funds through

community events and donations, they found themselves falling short of their target.

To make matters worse, they faced opposition from some members of the community who were

skeptical about the project's feasibility and impact. There were concerns about the environmental

impact of the center and its potential to disrupt the natural habitat of marine life in the area.

Adam and Emily knew that they needed to address these concerns head-on if they were to move

forward with their plans. They reached out to environmental experts and conducted studies to

assess the potential impact of the center on the local ecosystem. They also engaged in open

dialogue with community members, listening to their concerns and working to address them in a

transparent and responsible manner.

Despite their efforts, progress was slow, and Adam and Emily began to feel disheartened. It

seemed as though every step forward was met with two steps back, and they wondered if their

dream of a sea life center would ever become a reality.

But in the face of adversity, they refused to give up. They drew strength from their passion for

marine conservation and their unwavering belief in the importance of their mission. And with

each setback, they emerged more determined than ever to overcome the obstacles in their path

and see their vision through to fruition.

Chapter 10: A Beacon of Hope

Despite the challenges they faced, Adam and Emily remained steadfast in their commitment to
their vision. As they continued to work tirelessly towards the realization of the sea life center, they
began to see signs of progress and hope on the horizon.

One day, while attending a community meeting to discuss the project, they were approached by a
local philanthropist who had been following their efforts with interest. Moved by their dedication
and passion for marine conservation, the philanthropist offered to provide the funding needed to
kickstart the construction of the sea life center.

Adam and Emily were overcome with gratitude and relief. It was a turning point in their journey—a
beacon of hope that illuminated the path forward and reignited their belief in the possibility of
their dream becoming a reality.

With the support of the philanthropist's generous donation, Adam and Emily wasted no time in
getting to work. They assembled a team of architects, engineers, and environmental experts to
help bring their vision to life. Plans were drawn up, permits were obtained, and construction
crews were mobilized to begin work on the sea life center.

As the foundation for the center was laid, Adam and Emily felt a sense of excitement and

anticipation building within them. They knew that there would still be challenges ahead, but they

were more determined than ever to see their dream through to completion.

And as they looked out at the sea, shimmering in the sunlight, they couldn't help but feel a sense

of optimism for the future. The sea life center would not only be a place of education and

conservation but also a symbol of hope—a testament to what could be achieved when people

came together with a shared purpose and a commitment to making a difference.

Chapter 11: Tides of Change

As construction of the sea life center progressed, Adam and Emily found themselves swept up in a whirlwind of activity and excitement. Each day brought new developments and challenges, as

the once-empty plot of land transformed into a bustling hub of construction.

Despite their initial setbacks, Adam and Emily remained focused on their goal, drawing

inspiration from the progress being made and the support of the community. With each passing

day, the sea life center began to take shape, its sleek modern design rising from the ground like a beacon of hope against the backdrop of the sea.

But as the project neared completion, a new challenge emerged: a sudden change in government

regulations threatened to delay the opening of the sea life center indefinitely. Adam and Emily

were devastated by the news, fearing that their dream was slipping away from them once again.

However, they refused to let adversity defeat them. Drawing on their resilience and determination,

they mobilized their resources and launched a grassroots campaign to petition for the

regulations to be reconsidered.

Their efforts paid off, and after months of advocacy and negotiation, the regulations were amended, allowing the sea life center to proceed with its planned opening. Adam and Emily

breathed a sigh of relief, grateful for the opportunity to share their passion for marine

conservation with the world.

As the grand opening of the sea life center approached, Adam and Emily reflected on the journey

that had brought them to this moment. They had faced countless obstacles and challenges

along the way, but through perseverance and determination, they had emerged stronger and

more resilient than ever before.

And as they stood on the threshold of a new chapter in their lives, they knew that the tides of

change were finally turning in their favor. The sea life center was more than just a building—it was a testament to the power of hope, resilience, and the unwavering belief that together, we can

make a difference in the world.

Chapter 12: Weathering the Storm

As the grand opening of the sea life center approached, Adam and Emily were filled with a sense

of excitement and anticipation. Months of hard work and dedication were finally about to pay off,

and they couldn't wait to share their passion for marine conservation with the world.

But just as they were putting the finishing touches on the center, disaster struck in the form of an

unexpected storm. High winds and torrential rain lashed the coast, causing widespread damage

and destruction in its wake.

Adam and Emily watched in horror as the storm battered the sea life center, threatening to undo

all of their hard work in an instant. Despite their best efforts to secure the building, they knew

that there was only so much they could do in the face of such ferocious weather.

As the storm raged on, Adam and Emily huddled together, praying for the safety of their beloved

sea life center. When the worst of the storm had passed, they ventured outside to survey the

damage.

Their hearts sank as they took in the scene before them. The sea life center had sustained significant damage, with parts of the roof torn off and windows shattered by the force of the

wind. It was a devastating blow, and Adam and Emily felt as though their dreams were slipping

away from them once again.

But amidst the wreckage, they found a glimmer of hope. The structure of the sea life center was

still intact, and with the support of the community, they knew that they could rebuild and restore

what had been lost.

Drawing on their resilience and determination, Adam and Emily set to work repairing the damage

caused by the storm. With the help of volunteers and local contractors, they worked tirelessly to

make the sea life center even stronger than before.

And as they watched the sun rise on a new day, Adam and Emily knew that no storm could

extinguish their passion for marine conservation. Despite the setbacks they had faced, their

commitment to their dream remained unwavering, and they were more determined than ever to

see it through to fruition.

Chapter 13: A Beacon of Resilience

In the aftermath of the storm, Adam and Emily found themselves faced with the daunting task of

rebuilding the sea life center. But rather than succumbing to despair, they were determined to

turn the setback into an opportunity to demonstrate the resilience of their community.

With the support of volunteers and local contractors, Adam and Emily worked tirelessly to repair

the damage caused by the storm. Piece by piece, the sea life center began to take shape once

again, rising from the ashes like a phoenix reborn.

As news of their efforts spread, the community rallied around Adam and Emily, offering their

assistance and encouragement in any way they could. Together, they worked day and night to

ensure that the sea life center would be even stronger and more resilient than before.

But the rebuilding process was not without its challenges. Adam and Emily faced numerous

setbacks along the way, from shortages of materials to unforeseen complications in the

construction process. Yet, they refused to be deterred, drawing on their determination and

resolve to overcome each obstacle in their path.

Slowly but surely, the sea life center began to take shape once again, its walls rising higher with

each passing day. And as the grand reopening approached, Adam and Emily felt a sense of pride

and satisfaction knowing that they had weathered the storm and emerged stronger than ever

before.

The sea life center had become more than just a building—it was a symbol of resilience,

community, and the indomitable human spirit. And as its doors finally opened to the public once

again, Adam and Emily knew that their dream of creating a place where people could learn about and appreciate the wonders of the ocean was finally becoming a reality.

Chapter 14: Rebuilding Together

With the sea life center gradually taking shape again, Adam and Emily felt a renewed sense of

hope and purpose. But they knew that they couldn't complete the rebuilding process alone—they

needed the help of the entire community.

Drawing on the support of volunteers and local businesses, Adam and Emily organized a series

of community rebuilding events. From fundraising drives to volunteer workdays, the people of

Ramsey came together to lend a hand in any way they could.

Neighbors pitched in to help clean up debris and repair damaged buildings, while local

businesses donated supplies and services to support the rebuilding efforts. It was a true

testament to the strength and resilience of the community, as people from all walks of life came

together to support one another in their time of need.

As the weeks passed, the sea life center began to emerge from the rubble, its walls once again

standing tall against the backdrop of the sea. And with each brick laid and each window installed,

Adam and Emily felt a sense of gratitude for the community that had come together to support

their dream.

But the rebuilding process was about more than just restoring a building—it was about rebuilding

hope and resilience in the hearts of everyone who had been affected by the storm. And as the

sea life center took shape once again, Adam and Emily knew that they had played a part in

bringing their community closer together than ever before.

Chapter 15: Seeds of Resilience

As the sea life center nears completion, Adam and Emily reflect on the journey they've been on

since the storm. They've faced countless challenges and setbacks, but through it all, they've

discovered a strength and resilience they never knew they had.

The rebuilding process has been a test of their determination and perseverance, but it has also

brought them closer together as a couple and as members of the community. They've learned to

lean on each other for support and to rely on the kindness and generosity of their neighbors.

With the sea life center once again standing proud against the backdrop of the sea, Adam and

Emily feel a sense of pride and accomplishment. They know that their dream of creating a place

where people can learn about and appreciate the wonders of the ocean is finally becoming a

reality.

But they also know that their work is far from over. With the grand reopening just around the

corner, they're faced with the daunting task of preparing the sea life center to welcome visitors

once again. There are exhibits to set up, tanks to fill, and programs to plan—all while ensuring

that everything is done safely and responsibly.

Yet, despite the challenges that lie ahead, Adam and Emily are filled with hope for the future.

They know that the sea life center has the potential to be not just a place of education and

entertainment, but also a symbol of resilience and community spirit.

As they look out over the sea, Adam and Emily are filled with gratitude for the support they've

received from their friends, family, and neighbors. They know that it's thanks to the kindness and

generosity of others that they've been able to turn their dream into a reality, and they're

determined to pay that kindness forward in the days and weeks to come.

Chapter 16: Nurturing Dreams

With the sea life center rebuilt and preparations for the grand reopening underway, Adam and

Emily take a moment to reflect on the journey that has brought them to this point. They think

back to the early days, when their dream of creating a place where people could learn about and

appreciate the wonders of the ocean seemed like nothing more than a distant fantasy.

But now, as they stand on the brink of realizing that dream, they realize that it was their

determination, resilience, and unwavering belief in themselves and each other that brought them

here. They've overcome countless obstacles and setbacks along the way, but they've never lost

sight of what truly matters to them.

As they walk through the sea life center, admiring the exhibits and marveling at the diversity of

marine life on display, Adam and Emily feel a sense of pride and accomplishment wash over

them. They know that they've created something truly special—a place where people of all ages

can come together to learn, explore, and connect with the natural world.

But they also know that their work is far from over. With the grand reopening just days away, they're focused on making sure that everything is perfect for their guests. There are last-minute

details to attend to, exhibits to fine-tune, and staff to train—all while ensuring that the sea life

center is a safe and welcoming space for everyone who walks through its doors.

As they put the finishing touches on their preparations, Adam and Emily can't help but feel a

sense of excitement and anticipation. They know that the sea life center has the potential to

make a real difference in the lives of the people who visit it, and they're eager to see their dream

finally come to fruition.

But more than anything, they're grateful for the opportunity to share their passion for the ocean

with others. They know that it's thanks to the support of their friends, family, and community that

they've been able to make their dream a reality, and they're determined to make the most of it.

Chapter 17: Finding Strength

In the final days leading up to the grand reopening of the sea life center, Adam and Emily find

themselves faced with one final challenge. As they work tirelessly to put the finishing touches on

the exhibits and ensure that everything is ready for their guests, they can't shake the feeling of

unease that hangs over them.

The stress and pressure of the past few months have taken their toll, and Adam and Emily find

themselves struggling to keep up with the demands of their work. But just when they feel like

they're on the verge of breaking, they find strength in each other and in the support of their

friends and family.

Together, they rally their spirits and redouble their efforts, determined to overcome whatever

obstacles stand in their way. They know that the grand reopening is more than just a

celebration—it's a chance to showcase the resilience and determination of their community in the face of adversity.

As the big day draws near, Adam and Emily are filled with a sense of hope and anticipation. They know that the sea life center has the potential to bring joy and inspiration to countless people,

and they're determined to do everything in their power to make sure that the grand reopening is a success.

And as they stand side by side, ready to welcome their guests and share their passion for the

ocean with the world, Adam and Emily know that they've come a long way since the storm.

They've faced their fair share of challenges and setbacks, but through it all, they've never lost

sight of their dreams. And now, as they prepare to open the doors of the sea life center once

again, they know that anything is possible as long as they have each other.

Chapter 18: Rising Above

As the day of the grand reopening dawns, Adam and Emily are filled with a mix of excitement and

nervous anticipation. Months of hard work and determination have led to this moment, and they

can't help but feel a sense of pride in how far they've come.

With the sea life center sparkling and ready to welcome guests, Adam and Emily take a moment

to reflect on the journey that has brought them to this point. They think back to the storm that

nearly destroyed everything they had worked so hard to build and marvel at the resilience and

strength they've shown in the face of adversity.

But they also know that the grand reopening is about more than just celebrating their own

success—it's about celebrating the spirit of their community and the bonds that hold them all

together. As they look out at the crowd of smiling faces gathered outside the sea life center,

Adam and Emily feel a profound sense of gratitude for the support and encouragement they've

received from their friends, family, and neighbors.

As the doors of the sea life center swing open and the first guests begin to trickle in, Adam and

Emily feel a surge of emotion wash over them. They watch as children run excitedly from one exhibit to the next, their faces lighting up with wonder and awe at the sight of the colorful fish

and exotic sea creatures.

And as they walk through the sea life center, greeting guests and sharing stories about their

journey, Adam and Emily know that they've finally achieved their dream. They've created a place

where people can come together to learn, explore, and connect with the natural world, and they

couldn't be happier or more proud.

As the day draws to a close and the last of the guests begin to file out, Adam and Emily take a

moment to soak it all in. They know that there will be many more challenges and obstacles to

overcome in the days and weeks to come, but for now, they're content to bask in the glow of their success and celebrate the triumph of the human spirit.

Chapter 19: Into the Deep

With the grand reopening of the sea life center a resounding success, Adam and Emily find

themselves finally able to relax and enjoy the fruits of their labor. They take some time to wander

through the exhibits, marveling at the beauty and diversity of the marine life on display.

As they explore, they're approached by visitors who are eager to learn more about the sea

creatures and the work that went into creating the center. Adam and Emily are happy to share

their knowledge and passion with others, and they're thrilled to see how excited and engaged

their guests are.

But amidst the celebrations, Adam and Emily can't help but feel a sense of urgency about the

work that still lies ahead. They know that the sea life center is just the beginning of their journey

to make a difference in the world, and they're determined to continue pushing forward.

With plans already in motion for new exhibits and educational programs, Adam and Emily are

excited about the possibilities that lie ahead. They know that there's still so much work to be

done, but they're more determined than ever to make a positive impact on the world around them.

As they look out over the sea, Adam and Emily are filled with a sense of hope and possibility.

They know that the ocean is a vast and mysterious place, filled with wonders beyond

imagination, and they're eager to continue exploring its depths and sharing its beauty with others.

And as they stand together, hand in hand, they know that no matter what challenges may come

their way, they'll always have each other to rely on. With their love and determination as their

guide, they're ready to dive headfirst into the future, confident that together, they can overcome

anything that comes their way.

Chapter 20: Embracing Transformation

As Adam and Emily reflect on their journey, they realize that their lives have been transformed in

ways they never could have imagined. What started as a simple dream to create a sea life center

has blossomed into so much more—a testament to their resilience, determination, and

unwavering belief in the power of hope.

They think back to the challenges they've faced—the storm that threatened to destroy everything

they had worked so hard to build, the financial struggles, and the doubts and fears that crept in

along the way. But through it all, they never lost sight of their vision, or their love for each other.

And now, as they stand together on the shores of Ramsey, watching the sun set over the horizon,

they know that they've made it. They've built something truly special—a place where people can

come together to learn, explore, and connect with the natural world.

But more than that, they've built a life filled with love, purpose, and meaning. They've shown that

even in the darkest of times, there is always hope, and that with enough determination and

courage, anything is possible.

As they look out at the sea, Adam and Emily feel a sense of peace wash over them. They know that their journey is far from over, and that there will always be new challenges and adventures

waiting just beyond the horizon.

But whatever the future may hold, they're ready to face it together, hand in hand, with hearts full

of hope and dreams as big as the ocean itself. And as they take their first steps into this new

chapter of their lives, they know that the best is yet to come.

Chapter 21: A New Beginning

With the sea life center thriving and their dreams realized, Adam and Emily find themselves at a

crossroads. They've accomplished so much together, but they know that there are still new

adventures and challenges waiting to be explored.

As they sit down to talk about their future, they realize that they're ready for a new beginning.

They've spent years building their life in Ramsey, but now they're eager to see what else the world

has to offer.

After much discussion, they decide to embark on a new adventure, setting their sights on a

remote island where they can continue their work to protect and preserve the ocean and its

creatures.

With their hearts full of excitement and anticipation, Adam and Emily pack up their belongings

and say goodbye to Ramsey, knowing that they'll always carry a piece of it with them wherever

they go.

As they set sail for their new home, they're filled with a sense of optimism and possibility. They

know that the journey ahead won't be easy, but they're ready to face whatever challenges come

their way, together.

And as they look out at the vast expanse of the ocean stretching out before them, they know that

their love for each other and their passion for making a difference in the world will guide them on

this new adventure, just as it has guided them every step of the way

The Impact Chronicles

Look out for Woodys sealife adventures, where everyday is a new adventure on the sea.

The Impact Chronicles

The Impact Chronicles

The Impact Chronicles

The Impact Chronicles

Also by Paul Smith

The Impact Chronicles
Seeds of Change: A Journey to Ramsey
Roots of Resilience: Nurturing Change
Rising Tide: The Rebirth of Ramsey
Seeds of Renewal: Love's Everlasting Bloom

Watch for more at wix.pbsmith17@wix.com.

About the Author

Paul smith Artist, Aurthor & Designer. Island resident since 1999 Read more at wix.pbsmith17@wix.com.